THE SEARCH FOR ZANE

By Kate Howard

SCHOLASTIC INC.

ISBN 978-0-545-75054-7

12 11 10 9 8 7 6 5 4 3 2 1   15 16 17 18 19 20/0

Printed in the U.S.A.   40
This edition first printing, March 2015

CONTENTS

FROM THE JOURNAL OF

Sensei Garmadon

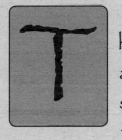hroughout Ninjago™, five ninja are well-known for their speed, strength, and — of course — the elemental powers that help them protect our world from evil. But there are others who possess some of the same powers as the ninja. Others who may not always use their powers for good.

Before now, the ninja believed they were special. They did not know there were others like them in the world. But in fact, there are many descendants of the original Elemental

Masters. Long ago, before Sensei Wu and I were born, the first Spinjitzu Master had guardians who were each endowed with an elemental power. These powers have been passed through generations. They need only be awoken for an individual's power to be fully realized.

Kai, Jay, Cole, Zane, and Lloyd all learned to harness their powers from my brother, Sensei Wu. They continue to learn from me. But many others have discovered their special talents on their own. They serve no master and have unlocked their powers without training.

The time has come for the ninja to meet some of the others who are like them.

Master Chen has invited the ninja to join him and the other descendants of the Elemental Masters at his Tournament of Elements. In this tournament, each player

will fight the others in one-on-one battles until a single victor emerges.

The ninja have agreed to attend Chen's tournament, but not in the quest for victory. Rather, Chen has led them to believe their missing friend, Zane, is alive and hidden somewhere on Chen's island.

Perhaps he is.

Perhaps he is not.

The ninja have traveled to Chen's island to search — and they hope to come back to the mainland as a complete team.

I swore to never return to Chen's island. But I have chosen to join the ninja at the tournament because Master Chen is a dangerous man. He should not be trusted. I know this because long ago, Chen was my sensei. When I was younger, I sought a darker means of guidance. Chen taught me to win at all costs, no matter who I hurt.

At one time, I considered Chen a friend. But during the Serpentine Wars — when my brother, Wu, and I fought side by side — Chen turned against his own kind and sided with the treacherous snakes. He used deception to divide the Elemental Masters. We barely defeated the Serpentine, and in a deal for his surrender, Chen was to never leave this island. Since then, he has built a criminal empire from his hidden island fortress. He is a Master of Dark Arts. And he is dangerously powerful.

The ninja serve with honor. But honor means nothing in Chen's tournament. The other fighters will be gunning for the ninja, and they will use any means necessary to win.

Though Lloyd, Kai, Jay, and Cole must all fight their own battles, I will be there to guide them. The ninja are in for many surprises with Master Chen, that much is certain.

I just hope they will find what they are looking for on Chen's island. I also hope that, without Zane by their side, they will find a way to prevail.

Sensei Garmadon

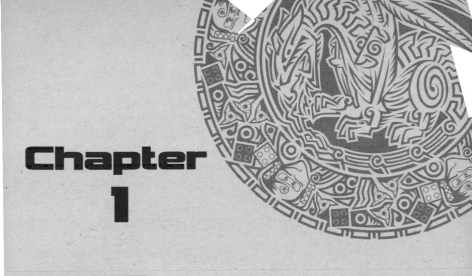

Chapter 1

Congratulations, Master of Fire."

Chen smiled at Kai. Sometimes Kai thought Chen looked much more like a friendly noodle shop owner than a Master of Dark Arts. Even though Chen *did* own a noodle shop — and they were seriously good noodles — the ninja couldn't be fooled. Not after Garmadon had told them some of the evil things Chen had done in the past.

Chen continued, "The Master of Fire has

moved on to the next round in my Tournament of Elements."

Kai breathed a sigh of relief. He, Jay, Cole, and Lloyd had all made it through their first challenge in Chen's tournament. The battle had been close, but the ninja had done what they needed to do to **stay in the game**. None of them could afford to lose this early in the competition.

If a player lost a challenge, they would get kicked off the island faster than you could say *egg roll*. And if any of the ninja got kicked off the island, they wouldn't get to look for Zane. That's what they were there for. They had to find their pal Zane, then get off Chen's creepy island and back to their day jobs: fighting evil, as a team.

Meanwhile, Kai's opponent, a metal-fisted warrior named Karlof, sulked. He had lost the tournament round to Kai, which meant he was out of the competition.

"Fine, I lose," Karlof said gruffly. He looked at Chen. "Karlof never wanted to be on stinking island anyway."

Master Chen's eyes flashed dangerously. "I'm sorry to hear you did not enjoy your stay. I guess this worked out for the best. This is good . . . BYE!"

In a flash, a trapdoor snapped open beneath Karlof, and he disappeared!

All of the competitors gasped. They knew losing meant you were out of the competition. But Chen had never said anything about trapdoors or **disappearing**. Where had Karlof gone? Where would *they* be sent to if they lost a tournament round?

All the Elemental Masters powered up, ready to fight! But Chen's guards quickly surrounded them.

"Tee-hee-hee!" Chen giggled, eerily cheerful. "As you can see, lose and you are out. Break any rule, you are out. Never bite the hand that feeds you . . . Master Chen's

delicious noodles! Now rest up! Tomorrow, the tournament will recommence!"

The four ninja looked at one another grimly. With Chen's guards surrounding them, they couldn't fight. They would have to continue in the tournament . . . or else.

But more important, they had to find Zane, and fast. They had seen the mad skills of the other Elemental Masters. There was no guarantee how long any of them would last in the competition.

And who knew what that meant?

Later, the friends met in Chen's temple cafeteria. They eyed the other competitors warily as they stood in line to get food. The other Elemental Masters eyed them in return.

"I'm starting to realize this isn't going to be as easy as we thought it would be, is it?" Kai asked.

"None of us can afford to lose," Lloyd said. "We have to find Zane —"

Jay cut him off. "And then we have to get out of here. This place gives me the creeps."

"I warned you," Sensei Garmadon said. "There's something fishy about Chen's tournament."

"Fishy?" Jay asked with a smile. "I thought you said Chen is into snakes?"

"*Was,*" Sensei Garmadon corrected him. "Long ago, he partnered with the Serpentine army. But that was many years ago."

Cole carried his tray of food to the table with his friends. "At least the chow's good here."

"It's killing me," Jay burst out suddenly. He couldn't stop thinking about how Kai's battle partner — Karlof — had disappeared down a trapdoor. "What's under the trapdoor? What happens when you lose?"

"Don't think about that," Garmadon said.

"It's *all* I can think about," Jay moaned. "I moved on. I feel guilt. These are not good feelings."

"You think *you* feel bad? Imagine how *I* feel. Karlof is out because of me." Kai sighed. "Now, our mission is simple. Tonight we find Zane and get off this crazy island."

"Just how are we supposed to do that?" Cole blurted. "You heard Chen. Break a rule, and we're out. He's not going to let us roam around."

"Then it's a good thing we're ninja." Kai smiled knowingly. "Meet in my room at midnight."

The friends stood to leave the cafeteria, but Lloyd looked pensive.

"What's bugging you?" Jay demanded.

"Why are we waiting until tonight? We have all day to search for Zane, and we're going to do what? Take warm baths and relax for the next few hours?" Lloyd said.

Jay's cheeks turned red. That was exactly what he had in mind. "Uh, no?"

"Exactly," said Lloyd. "We need to get moving. Now."

Cole shook his head. "But how are we supposed to sneak around the island in broad daylight? Chen's guards are swarming the whole place."

"Like Kai said, we're *ninja*," Lloyd insisted. "We're trained to be sneaky."

Jay gestured to Cole's rumbling stomach. "No one's going to be sneaking anywhere with Cole. We might as well just tell Chen where we're going. 'Hey, Noodle Dude, check out Cole's stomach tunes!'"

"Enough," Garmadon said, quieting the group. "I agree with Lloyd and Kai. If we're going to act, we must act quickly. The more time spent on this island, the **greater danger** we are all in."

Chapter 2

The ninja decided to split into two groups to make their escape from Chen's heavily guarded fortress. They knew that a group of two or three sneaking out would attract a lot less attention than all five of them walking out together.

"Lloyd, why don't you come with me?" Kai suggested. "Jay, Cole, you go with Sensei Garmadon, and we'll meet outside the front gate in a couple of minutes."

"I'm going with Lloyd," Garmadon insisted.

Lloyd was Garmadon's son. They had only been reunited for a short while, and Garmadon liked to stay close by Lloyd whenever he could.

"Fine," Kai said. "Guys?" He looked at the other ninja.

Cole and Jay stared at each other. Neither wanted to work together. They were still having a hard time getting along because of Kai's sister, Nya. Things always got messy when two guys fell for the same girl. After a long moment, Cole moved away from Jay and said, "Ah, um —"

"You two *still* can't get along?" Lloyd asked. "When are you going to get over it?"

"When Nya finally realizes I'm the **best guy** for her," Jay said.

Cole scoffed. "Even though the computer test she took said *I* was her perfect match. Why don't I go with Lloyd and Sensei, and Kai can team up with Jay?"

"Fine, whatever," Kai said. "We're not picking teams for soccer. It's just our exit strategy. Come on, Jay, let's get moving."

The first group of two ninja snuck through the large front entrance of the palace. Jay and Kai tried not to attract any attention from Chen's guys. Large, muscled guards were clustered all around the palace courtyard. Chen's island was practically swimming with them — and they had all been tasked with making sure no one broke the rules.

Also, Chen's sinister assistant, Clouse, was lurking around. He and Garmadon clearly had some kind of history. Clouse seemed especially interested in the ninja.

The most distracting part of their whole escape plan, though, was the Kabuki entertainers. They were like creepy clowns who pranced around the courtyard acting as Master Chen's jesters. They danced and mimed and had the habit of popping up unexpectedly at any moment.

Jay and Kai pressed their backs against the rough fortress walls. They ducked under small trees and shrubs every time one of the guards looked their way. "Get down, Jay," Kai whispered as a pair of guards came close. They continued to slither along the edge of the wall until they could see the big gate. It was shut tight.

"NOW what?" Jay asked. He and Kai were crouched behind a leafy tree that someone had trimmed into the shape of a pelican. "Think if I yell 'Open sesame,' the gates will magically open?"

"We're going to have to wait until they have a reason to open the gate," Kai said. "I wish Zane were here. He'd be able to calculate the probability of the gate opening and the exact moment we should go."

Jay picked up one of the rocks lining the edge of a garden. He passed it from one hand to the other. "I have an idea. We need to trick the guards into thinking there's

someone outside the gates. Grab a couple of rocks, and get ready to toss them. We're going to make some noise on the *other* side of the wall."

Kai and Jay both picked up rocks and began to toss them over the high wall. *"Hi-yahh!"* Kai said softly. The rocks went sailing over the wall. As they fell to the ground, they knocked branches off trees and boomed onto the earth on the other side. The guards gathered at the gate all **snapped to attention**

"Who's out there?" one demanded.

"Announce yourself!" shouted another.

The two ninja looked at each other, surprised.

"I've got to admit, I didn't think that would actually work," confessed Jay.

The guards opened the gate and cautiously stepped out of the courtyard to investigate. They left the front entrance unguarded — for just one second too long.

As soon as the coast was clear, Jay and Kai dashed through the open gates and ran for cover on the other side.

Meanwhile, Cole, Lloyd, and Garmadon had taken a different approach for their escape. They scaled the impossibly high walls that protected the fortress and stealthily ran along the edge.

Off in the distance, Cole, Lloyd, and Garmadon could see the courtyard gates opening — for Jay and Kai. "I guess we could have just used the front gate," muttered Cole.

"That would have been too easy," said Lloyd.

"You ready to jump?" Cole asked. His stomach **rumbled** loudly — luckily, they were high enough that none of the guards below could hear. He'd have to do something really foolish, like yelling, to attract someone's attention way up there. Cole looked out at the leafy trees that surrounded the courtyard. A few yards out, he

spotted a branch that he hoped could support his weight. "We'll go on three. One, two —"

Lloyd leaped on two. But he didn't jump far enough. Instead of making it to a branch, he fell. Down, down, down.

Splat!

"Lloyd!" Cole yelled. He covered his mouth when he realized he'd probably gotten more attention than he'd bargained for. Just as one of the guards looked up to see what the commotion was, Cole said, "Three," and he and Garmadon jumped.

Chapter 3

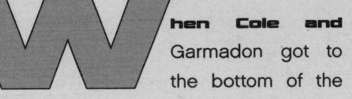

When Cole and Garmadon got to the bottom of the tree, Lloyd was moaning on the ground.

"Are you okay?" Garmadon asked, kneeling beside his son.

"I'm fine," Lloyd said, brushing himself off. "I guess you could say I took the direct route."

As soon as he was certain Lloyd was okay, Garmadon said, "We should get out of this area as quickly as possible."

"Sensei's right," said Cole, just as Kai and Jay ran up. "Great, now we're all here. Let's

head this way and start exploring the island. Zane's got to be here somewhere."

The ninja ran quickly away from Chen's fortress, hoping the guards were far behind them. Soon, they found themselves in a thickly wooded area. The trees were lush, providing good cover for renegade ninja who were exploring in an area they weren't supposed to be. The ground was covered with moss and leaves, masking their footsteps. The branches above their heads made it almost seem like it was nighttime outside, though the midday sun was shining brightly above the trees.

"We need to get to higher ground," said Kai. "If we could scan the whole island, we'd be able to see where Chen may be keeping Zane."

"Good idea, Kai," said Cole. He pointed to a path leading upward through the thick groves of trees. "Let's go that way."

As they walked, Jay looked around at the wooded surroundings. "You know, if it weren't for the **creepy clown dancers** ... and the maniacal host ... and the temple of doom ... this island would be a pretty relaxing vacation spot."

"Be quiet," Cole said urgently.

"It was just a joke, Cole," hissed Jay.

"No, seriously — *shh*. I think I hear something." Cole held up his hand for silence. "It's water. I hear running water."

"You think it's a river or something?" asked Kai.

Garmadon nodded and closed his eyes thoughtfully. "Many years ago, I trained on this island. I do remember a river, long and winding." He opened his eyes. "And a waterfall. There is a waterfall."

"Then I think we should check it out," said Lloyd. "Where there's a waterfall, there's also a cliff that the water can fall over. It will be a

25

good place to get a view of the island. Let's go."

They made their way toward the sound of running water. After a few hundred yards, they came to a wide river flowing quickly. "I'm starting to realize Chen's island is bigger than we may have thought," said Kai.

"Guys!" exclaimed Lloyd. "What's that — out there in the middle of the river?" Lloyd pointed. The others followed his gaze. There were several **huge rocks** jutting up out of the middle of the river.

"They call them *rocks*," said Jay, cracking himself up.

"I mean, what's *on* the rocks? Do you see that?" Lloyd ran forward to the river edge. He stepped into the water and the current rushed past so quickly that it nearly washed him away.

"Lloyd, be cautious!" Garmadon urged. "You must choose your path wisely."

26

"There's some sort of symbol on the big rock in the middle of the river," Lloyd exclaimed. "I'm going out there to check it out. It might be some sort of **clue** about the island. Maybe even about Zane."

"It's too dangerous," warned Garmadon. "The current is too strong."

Lloyd wasn't about to be stopped by *water*. He was the Green Ninja! He could handle some harmless water, no problem. He jumped from the shore onto a small rock a few feet away. The others gathered at the edge to watch him.

Lloyd easily leaped from one rock to the next, making it look as though he were fol-lowing an official path into the middle of the river. When he was almost to the large rock, he stopped and waved at the others. "Almost there!" he called. As he turned back, he slipped. *"Whoa!"* He waved his arms around in circles, trying to catch his balance.

"Don't fall in!" Cole hollered.

Kai, Jay, and Garmadon all watched nervously. Time stood still for a moment as Lloyd continued to windmill his arms. Just when they thought it was all over, Lloyd righted himself and leaped to the next rock. The other ninja breathed sighs of relief.

"And you thought I was going to fall," Lloyd called back to shore, grinning. He turned and leaped again, and that's when it happened: The corner of his foot caught a patch of slippery moss on the edge of the rock. **Splash!** Lloyd was in the river! The current dragged him downstream!

"We have to get him!" Cole cried, running along the shoreline. The river was fast — if they didn't hurry, they'd lose him.

"Where did he go?" Jay yelled. "I can't see him anymore." The ninja all ran, but Lloyd had disappeared.

Just then, Lloyd's head bobbed above

the surface of the water for a second. But he was pulled down again. "He's there," shouted Kai, pointing into the middle of the river. He yelled to Lloyd, but he wasn't sure if his friend could hear him over the rushing water. "Lloyd, there's a rock up ahead — try to grab it!"

Again, Lloyd's head broke through the surface of the water. He reached out, and *yes*! He wrapped his arms around the rock and held on. The water was still tugging at him, but Lloyd held tight.

"We need something long so we can pull him back to shore," yelled Cole. He scanned the forested shoreline. "There! Grab that branch."

Kai dragged a long tree branch over to shore. The ninja and Sensei Garmadon took hold of it, grabbing it tight as they stretched it out toward the center of the river. When it was near enough, Lloyd reached out his hand and held fast. The rushing water pulled

at his body as they tried to bring him back toward safety. It was almost like they'd caught a fish on a line, but instead of a fish, this was *Lloyd* they were reeling in.

"The water is too powerful," yelled Kai. "It's tugging Lloyd harder than we are. We're going to lose him."

"We need one more person to help," said Jay.

"We need Zane," said Cole.

"Pull!" urged Garmadon.

But the water was too much for even the ninja to handle. The branch began to give way under the water's pressure. The ninja pulled harder, but the river pulled back. Suddenly, the ninja felt *themselves* being yanked forward in a mighty surge.

Splish! Splash!

"*Ayeeeee!*" Jay cried as he hit the water. He was tossed under the surface. Just in time, his head popped up and he took

a huge gulp of air. Then he saw something that made his breath catch again. "Guys . . ." he exclaimed as he saw where the water was taking them. "I think we found the waterfall!"

Chapter 4

Ahhhhh!" the ninja all screamed. The river was quickly carrying them straight toward the giant waterfall.

Moments before they toppled over the edge, Cole spotted a long vine trailing down into the water. He reached out and grabbed hold of it. It nearly slipped through his fingers, but he held fast. As the rest of the ninja came bobbing toward him through the rushing water, he shouted, "Grab on!"

Kai grabbed on. Then Jay, Lloyd, and finally Sensei Garmadon. The river continued to pull them toward the plunging waterfall, but the team didn't let go. The vine slipped a bit, and they all shot closer to the falls again. Sensei Garmadon's legs were now dangling over the edge of the waterfall — the strength of the team holding tight was the only thing keeping him from plunging to the bottom.

From here, they could easily see more of Chen's island. It was *huge*, and the drop off the waterfall was really **scary-looking**.

"So," Jay yelled to Garmadon after a moment, "how's it hanging?"

"Jay," Kai growled. "This is not a time for jokes."

"Okay," said Cole. "What are we going to do now?"

"It's not like we can hope someone finds us here and comes to our rescue," said Lloyd. "I think the only thing worse than *this* is the possibility we might get caught by Chen's guards."

The vine gave way again. When it did, the water pulled the whole line of ninja forward. Now they were *all* hanging off the edge of the cliff. The only thing below them was foaming water and jagged rocks.

"*Now* can I ask how it's hanging?" asked Jay. The vine gave some more, and the ninja slipped down a little farther. "Is it just me, or does it seem like this is this one seriously long vine?"

"I don't know how much longer I can hold on," Cole said, wincing.

The water bounced the ninja to and fro, making it harder and harder for them to hold on. "I don't know about the rest of you," said Kai. "But I'm thinking we should just —" His voice cut off as the vine suddenly snapped and sent them all plunging down into the hissing water below. "Drop!" he yelled.

Their bodies twisted and turned in midair. Jay hollered all the way down. At the bottom, the five ninja hardly made a splash as they

plunged into the raging waters. After what felt like an eternity, all of them spluttered to the surface again, coughing and gasping.

"Everyone alive?" Jay asked, scanning the bubbling surface of the water for the others.

One by one, everyone else answered yes. After a few deep breaths, the team swam toward the sandy shoreline.

"Well," said Cole. "So much for getting a good view of the island from the top of the waterfall."

"I saw enough to realize just how huge Chen's mysterious island is," said Kai. "Searching for Zane here is like looking for a **needle in a haystack**."

"Well," said Lloyd, wringing out the bottom of his gi. "We need to try. Zane's relying on us. We have to find him if we want to be a complete team again."

"Lloyd, did you get a closer look at the symbols on the rock in the river?" asked Kai.

Lloyd shook his head. "I fell in before I could get a good look."

The others sat quietly for a moment, considering their next move. Cole got up to pace. "Okay, so here's what we know: The island is huge, Chen's guards are everywhere, and Lloyd can't walk on water."

Lloyd glared at him.

"What we need is some sort of clue," said Kai.

Cole stopped and stared into the **dark area** beneath the waterfall. Over the years, the rushing water had carved out a cave-like space behind the falling water. "Uh, you guys? Anyone want to take a guess at what *that* is?"

The others hustled over to stand beside Cole.

"That?" asked Garmadon. He stepped forward and reached out his hand. Whatever Cole had found was leathery, but delicate-looking. It was almost like an enormous pile

of rice paper, stacked up in a heap. It was huge — longer than all the ninja put together, and nearly as wide. Garmadon broke off a piece and took it in his hand. "That is a snakeskin."

"A snakeskin?" gasped the others, rushing forward.

"That has to be the skin from one *big* snake," said Jay.

"Right," said Cole. "And if the skin is here . . . where's the snake?"

Suddenly, a loud boom rang out on the other side of the waterfall. A moment later, several groups of people came into view. They hadn't yet seen the ninja, but in just a few moments, they would.

"I don't know about a snake," said Kai. "But I think I see something worse: Chen's guards. Everyone, run!"

Chapter 5

hatever you all do, don't let them see you," warned Sensei Garmadon.

"We *cannot* get caught," Cole agreed. "If we do, then everything's over, including our search for Zane."

The ninja dashed across the riverbed and dove behind some huge rocks. When they peeked out from their hiding spots, they could see Chen's guards were everywhere.

"How did they find us?" Kai asked as they all watched the guards warily.

Cole's stomach rumbled again.

"Well, there's a clue," muttered Jay.

"Or maybe it was all your screaming-like-a-baby when we fell off the waterfall?" Cole snapped back.

"You need to work as a team if we're going to escape," Garmadon reminded them.

"My dad's right," said Lloyd. "We need to stop bickering and remember why we're here. We need to get moving and see if we can find any more clues that could **lead us to Zane**."

Quickly, the ninja zigzagged past the boulders that surrounded the bottom of the waterfall. When they were sure they were safely out of sight, they ran — away from the waterfall and the giant snakeskin and Chen's guys.

Cole looked up at the sky. "It's getting later in the day," he said. "We need to be back to the temple before dinner, or the others will notice we're missing."

"Maybe we should split up, and then we could cover more ground?" suggested Kai.

Garmadon shook his head. "I don't think it's a good idea to split up. It's too dangerous."

"The island is too big, and together, we're wasting time," said Cole. "We have a better chance of finding Zane if we split into two groups."

"Fine by me," said Jay. "Same groups as before, though."

"What if someone finds something?" asked Kai.

Cole shrugged. "Should we have some sort of signal?"

"Caw like a bird." Jay flapped his arms and crowed, **"Caw! Caw!"**

Cole and Lloyd walked away from him, shaking their heads. "Good luck *not* getting caught," said Cole. They hustled up a hill with Garmadon trailing after them.

Jay spun in a slow circle. *"Sooooo . . ."*

"Where to?" asked Kai.

"What we really need right about now," Jay said thoughtfully, "are **dragons**! A sweet ride that would get us up and over the tree line. Think of how much ground we could cover if we had vehicles or dragons to show us around."

Kai shrugged. "Well, we don't have drag-ons, so . . ."

"So we walk," sighed Jay. They set off, walking away from the river along the bottom of the long ridge of rock their friends had just set off to climb. As they walked, Jay talked. He kept scanning their surroundings for things he could use to build a vehicle or some sort of search tool. Kai tuned him out, hoping they would find something soon that would make his buddy stop talking.

He was in luck. Ahead, there was a large black bird sitting on top of one of the rock formations. It seemed to be staring at Kai and Jay as they made their way along the bottom of the rock face.

"Hey, Jay, is that a real bird?" Kai said, pointing toward the creature. "Look at how its eyes follow our every move."

Jay stared up at the bird. He waved his arms in the air, then dashed back and forth — the bird's head swiveled back and forth, back and forth. He danced, and still the bird watched him. "I think it likes us."

Kai wasn't so sure. "What if it's not a real bird? What if it's some sort of **robo-spy** that Chen planted out here to keep an eye on the remote parts of his island? Maybe the bird has a camera inside, and it's projecting our every move back to Chen and Clouse at the palace."

Jay stopped dancing back and forth. "If it is, then I just made a pretty big fool of myself." He paused. "Do you really think it could be a robot?"

"With Chen, anything's possible. We should be careful." Kai walked on, searching

their surroundings for any signs of life or clues.

A few minutes later, Jay said, "The bird's still following us." In fact, it was. The bird had flown along the top of the ridge, and now sat perched on another rocky post. When Jay stopped to stare at it, the bird cawed at him. He cocked his head. "You don't think the bird is trying to get our attention, do you?"

Kai looked at him like he was crazy. "Uh, no."

"Think about it. You know how Zane is with birds. They love the guy. What if that bird knows where he is, and he's trying to get us to follow him?" Jay shrugged his shoulders. "It's possible."

Sighing, Kai admitted, "I guess it is possible."

"I say we head up the cliff and follow it. It's the best lead we've gotten all day." Jay began to scramble up the side of the rocky

cliff. It was tough going, but he and Kai were both able to find enough foot- and hand-holds that they were soon nearly halfway up the steep rock face.

"Almost there," grunted Kai, pulling himself up so he was level with Jay. The bird was still sitting serenely at the top of the cliff, watching their every move. Up close, it was easy to see that it was very much a real bird and not a robot. Both guys were hopeful that maybe they had found a clue that would help lead them to Zane.

"If it's still there when we get to the top, we know it's waiting for us," Jay said, grabbing for a jagged chunk of rock. He heaved himself upward again. Then he put his foot on a small rocky ledge and stopped for a rest. The only warning that something was wrong came when the bird spread its wings, squawked several times, and took flight. Less than a second later, the rock under Jay's feet broke away from the cliff and plummeted to

the ground below. Jay was dangling by his hands, and he couldn't see any more places he could put his feet.

In the next instant, more rocks pulled away from the face of the cliff and began tumbling past the two ninja. It was a **rockslide**! The wall boomed around them as rocks clattered and fell and thudded to the ground below. Both Jay and Kai were hanging — helpless — from the side of a cliff.

And if they screamed for help, there was a very real chance Chen's guards would find them long before their friends did.

Chapter 6

What are we going to do?" asked Kai.

The bird cawed again, from high up in the sky, before flapping away.

"So much for following the bird," said Jay. "I say we try to figure out how we get the rest of the way up rather than following the rocks back down."

Both ninja could feel the rock face crumbling all around them. "Whatever we do, we need to do it fast — or we're not going to have much of a say in the matter." As soon as Kai spoke, the rock under his left hand gave way and he swung down.

It was almost **impossible** to see anything around them, since there were so many rocks tumbling at them from above. They were in big trouble, and there was no easy way out of their situation. They needed a miracle.

Suddenly, a voice rang out from far overhead. "Kai! Look to your left — there's another rock just a couple of inches up that you can grab."

It was Cole!

Kai did as he was told, and soon he was holding on to the rock face with both hands again. He took a deep breath and called, "Thanks, Cole."

"If you reach up a little farther with your right leg, Jay, you'll find a spot to rest your foot," said Lloyd.

Step by step, Cole, Lloyd, and Garmadon helped Jay and Kai find their way up the rock

face as the wall continued to crumble around them. When they were finally at the top, Kai asked, "How did you know to come find us?"

"You cawed," said Cole. "That was our signal, right?"

Jay laughed. "It *was* our signal! But that wasn't me cawing like a bird — it was an actual bird. We were following it."

"You were following it?" asked Lloyd.

Jay and Kai looked at each other a bit sheepishly. Now that the bird was gone, their lead suddenly seemed a little silly. Still, though . . .

"I can't explain it, but the bird reminded me of . . . Zane," Jay said slowly. "And its cawing did save us. Kind of like he was here watching out for us, you know?"

The ninja looked at one another, slightly **spooked**.

"Maybe we should stick together from now on," Lloyd suggested. "Come on. My dad said he remembered a temple garden

in the direction we were heading, from when he trained on the island. We were going to go check it out when we heard, you know, the caw."

They walked for about a mile. The ground was uneven, and it made the trek difficult. All the ninja were growing tired, but they knew they only had a **few hours** left to search, so they continued on.

Soon, they came upon a beautiful garden. Bright flowers bloomed everywhere, and small, delicate-looking trees lined the space. There was a bubbling fountain in the center of the garden that made the space sound peaceful and relaxing.

"I *hope* we find Zane here," Jay said. "Because this would not be a terrible place for him to have had to spend some time."

The ninja all walked around the garden, searching for any sign of life — or their missing friend. "This bench is all dirty," said Jay, running his finger over a stone seat. When

he lifted it again, it was covered with gray dust. "I'm getting the impression that no one has spent time in this garden for a while. I wonder if Chen even knows this is here?"

"I'm pretty sure he does," said Cole. "And I'm starting to think Chen is the kind of guy who doesn't like to share his pretty things. Look." Cole was pointing at a long metal rod that was tucked under leaves along one edge of the garden. The rod was connected to a pulley system that, when triggered, would snap up an unsuspecting victim in a **mechanical trap**.

"He set *traps* in his garden?" asked Lloyd. "As if the guy doesn't have enough space out here on his island that he can't share some of the flowers with others?"

"We must walk carefully," said Garmadon. "Where there is one trap, there are likely many more."

Kai nodded. "And I'd also say that where there are traps, there is probably something

50

Chen is trying to hide. What's the point of booby trapping this place if he's not hiding something?"

"That is an excellent point," said Cole. "Clearly, Chen is up to no good in this garden. Let's split up and search. We'll see if anyone can find clues that might help us get closer to Zane."

The ninja all headed off in different directions, scanning the ground and the garden for any sign of evil activity. "Guys, I think I found something! It's another symbol." Lloyd's voice rang out from the far northwest corner of the garden. The other ninja set off at a run.

When they reached Lloyd, the ninja all stared at the symbol. It was the emblem of a large, **ominous snake** carved into a round, flat stone in the ground.

"Another snake?" asked Jay. "All this snake talk is starting to give me the *slithers*."

His friends groaned. But Garmadon had grown strangely quiet.

"This may be worse than I feared," he said. "I know this symbol. Perhaps it is left over from long ago. And yet . . . we must leave. Now."

"Hang on a sec." Kai studied the symbol closer. "I think I've seen this before."

"You have?" the others asked.

Kai nodded. "Yeah, actually, in my room. I thought it was just some sort of decoration. But there was definitely a drawing that looked like this hanging on the wall near my bed."

"Do you think they're connected?" Lloyd asked. "There was a symbol by the river, and that's where we found the snakeskin. And now a symbol here. If there's one in your bedroom, Kai, then maybe . . ."

Jay groaned. "Then maybe we should have all just planned to meet in Kai's room at midnight like he originally said!"

Suddenly, there was a **snap**, then a **thud** behind the ninja! Jay and

Cole whipped around just in time to see Sensei Garmadon being swept off his feet by one of Chen's garden traps!

"Dad!" cried Lloyd.

"I'm okay!" Garmadon insisted. But the sensei was stuck **upside down** inside a large, clawlike trap. It looked like a giant metal Venus flytrap had snapped closed around his body.

"Jay, I think *now* is probably a better time to ask Sensei how it's hanging," said Kai.

"You stole my joke," muttered Jay.

"Quit kidding around," said Lloyd. "We need to figure out how we're going to get my dad down."

"Chen probably has his traps hooked up to sensors of some kind," added Cole. "His guards might be on their way right now. We have to free Sensei and move on as fast as we can."

Garmadon shook his head. "Don't worry about me. Leave now, before you're caught."

Lloyd shook his head vehemently. "No way! We're not leaving without you. We're sticking together as a team. **No more splitting up!**"

Kai and Jay studied the giant metal claw. The sensei was held in tightly, and it would take a lot of strength to twist the metal and to free him.

"If Zane were here, he could probably freeze the claw and shatter it," mused Jay.

Cole flexed his arms. "Well, we don't have ice, so time to use our muscles."

The ninja all set to work tugging and pulling at each of the metal arms wrapped around Garmadon. When it was clear they were making no progress working alone, Kai said, "Maybe if we all pull on the same metal arm-thingy, we can get it to budge?"

Jay shrugged. "Can't hurt to try."

The four ninja all clasped their hands around one of the metal arms holding Garmadon prisoner. It took a lot of grunting, and even more muscle power, but eventually, the metal began to twist.

As they tugged more, Kai asked, "Do you think Chen sets these traps here to catch *people* wandering around his garden . . . or to catch animals?"

"Maybe he's trying to catch the giant snake who left his skin back at the river," Cole suggested, grunting.

Jay nodded. "Maybe giant snake is the secret ingredient in Chen's noodles."

"Let's not think about that," said Lloyd. "We have to eat here through the rest of the tournament."

The bar bent a few inches farther. But before the opening was wide enough to pull Garmadon out of his trap, voices echoed near the edge of the garden.

"Someone's coming," Garmadon hissed urgently. "You must go."

"We're not leaving you!" the ninja insisted.

The voices drew nearer. Soon, the ninja could make out what they were saying:

"Chen's instructions are to deliver the trespassers directly to him."

Chapter 7

Kai and Lloyd shared a worried glance. They just had to pull a little bit more, and then the metal arm would be loose enough for the sensei to squeeze through.

"I'm going to use Spinjitzu," said Lloyd, his face set. "I can get this trap opened in no time."

"No, Lloyd, don't," Cole urged. "If you use your powers, they'll spot it. That would be the end of our search for Zane."

Lloyd gritted his teeth and tugged harder.

"On the count of three, we give it one more good pull," said Cole. "One, two —" With one final tug from the four of them, the metal bent and scraped, and a moment later the sensei was free. He spun in the air and dropped to the ground lightly. Then the ninja and Garmadon shot out of the garden like a flash.

As they ran, Cole huffed, "Is anyone ever gonna wait for *three* again? Or do we just go on *two* now?"

They ran and ran, until their lungs burned and they were sure they'd put plenty of distance between themselves and Chen's thugs.

"Clearly, we need to be more careful," said Kai. "We're no closer to finding Zane, but we keep getting a *lot* closer to getting ourselves **kicked off the island** We can't afford any more mistakes."

"We must focus," said Garmadon. "Let's think about what we've learned."

"Here's what we've learned," said Jay. "Lloyd keeps finding weird symbols, vines

are super-stretchy in this place, cliffs are not our friends but birds are, and we need to check our noodles for chunks of snake. Is that a good recap of the day?"

Kai shook his head. "We also discovered the symbols connecting back to my room. Maybe we've been going about this all wrong. Maybe we don't need to be searching outside the fortress for Zane. Maybe we need to be searching **inside** it."

Lloyd gasped. "You're right! Chen's fortress is massive, but we've only seen a small section of it. What if Zane's somewhere in there, right under our noses?"

Suddenly, the ninja heard a loud *Caw! Caw!* above them. They looked up and spotted the black bird from before. It circled once, its shadow blocking the sunlight over them. Then it flew off.

"It's getting late," Kai realized. "If we don't get back soon, they're sure to spot that we're missing."

"So does that mean we're going back to the fortress?" asked Cole. "Time to sneak back in?"

"I don't think we have much choice," said Jay.

As they hurried back toward the fortress, Cole was strangely quiet. "We had a couple of close scrapes there," he finally said. "We sure could have used Zane's help today."

"I know," said Lloyd. "I never realized how much we relied on one another until we lost Zane."

"I think it's safe to say that **finding Zane** would be a lot easier if Zane were here to help," agreed Jay.

"Very interesting," murmured Garmadon. "Though you did not find your friend yet, you have found something almost as important. The value of your team."

The others nodded. Jay said, "Cheesy as it is, Sensei's right. Now I want to find Zane

even more than I did when we first got here. We *have* to find him tonight."

Soon, the friends could see the fortress stretching high into the sky up ahead. The walls were just as solid as they had been earlier in the day, but this time, the front gates were wide open. The entire area near the gates was filled with Chen's guards. In the courtyard, **Kabuki performers** were dancing and miming near the palace steps, trying to entertain everyone. Elsewhere around the courtyard, other competitors prepared for their next battles.

Griffen Turner, who had superspeed, was punching at the air so fast his hands looked like a blur. The Pale Man, who could turn himself invisible, was winding in and out of the crowd. Kai watched him for a minute, then said, "That guy's power sure would come in handy right about now."

Lloyd stopped short and said, "That's one thing we didn't think about . . . How are we going to get back in without anyone noticing we were gone in the first place?"

"There are a lot of people in there," said Cole, stating the obvious.

Kai nodded. "A lot of people who would love to see us get kicked out of the competition."

Jay's face broke into a smile. "I think I have an idea — follow me."

Chapter 8

This is so embarrassing," Kai said a few minutes later.

"You look good," giggled Jay. "We all do. Especially Sensei. Clown suits suit you."

Garmadon frowned. "This had *better* work."

The ninja had snuck around the outside of the fortress wall and found the room that held the Kabuki performers' costumes. Now, all five of them were dressed in the colorful outfits. They had also found makeup to paint their faces, so they were totally masked as

they slowly made their way toward the front gates.

"Act silly," ordered Jay, nudging the others. "The Kabuki are like Chen's jesters, remember — we need to make sure we're playing the part right."

"This is the worst part of this whole day," growled Kai. Though he was angry, his face looked cheerful because of his painted-on smile.

"I much prefer my ninja gi," agreed Cole.

"Let's just get this over with," said Lloyd, and he walked right up to the front gates.

None of the guards seemed to notice them. They danced and mimed around the courtyard, trying to act like they fit in. Several of the other Kabuki performers gave them strange looks, but before long, they'd made it most of the way across the courtyard without anyone saying anything to them at all.

Suddenly, Chen and Clouse stepped out of the front doors. Everyone in the courtyard

froze when they saw them. The ninja all held their breath — surely, Chen would notice that something was strange about his newest Kabuki performers! Chen strolled across the courtyard, looking very much like a king in his castle.

The ninja backed away from him, but Chen and Clouse just kept coming closer.

"You!" Chen barked, looking right at Garmadon. **"Make me laugh!"**

Garmadon paused a moment too long. Chen narrowed his eyes, and Clouse stepped closer to the sensei.

"This is bad . . ." Jay muttered. He tried to think of a backup plan, but nothing was coming to mind.

Just as Chen stepped forward, putting him a foot away from Garmadon, the sensei began to dance. He was almost completely unrecognizable in his Kabuki outfit with a face full of makeup. And his dancing . . .

"He's not bad!" Cole whispered to Kai.

Kai smiled. "Not bad at all."

Garmadon's feet flopped back and forth in a silly little **dance**, and he waved his arms like he'd seen the other Kabuki doing earlier. Chen's eyes narrowed further.

"He's not falling for it," groaned Lloyd.

Then, Chen began to laugh. *"Tee-hee-hee!"* He cried, "Wonderful!" Then he walked on, Clouse trailing at his heels.

As soon as Chen had passed them, the ninja hurried toward the front steps. They ran inside and dashed through the hallways to the guest rooms. They all dodged into Lloyd's room, because it was the closest. Inside, they cast off their Kabuki outfits and breathed heavy sighs of relief.

"We made it back without getting caught," said Kai.

"We did," said Lloyd, looking up at a picture on his wall. Lloyd's room had a framed painting of all five ninja — back when they were still a team, and before Zane was gone.

"We'll find him," said Jay. "Remember, we're meeting tonight."

"See you at midnight?" asked Kai. "My room?"

Garmadon nodded. "Yes. You four meet, and I shall keep a lookout for Chen and Clouse to make sure you are not discovered," he said. "Seeing you work as a team today gave me great hope that you will find Zane. Good luck tonight, ninja. Let the spirit of your brother Zane give you the strength to search on."

The others nodded back. Then they quietly headed to their own chambers. They had to rest up — they still had a lot of searching left to do.

Chapter 9

t midnight, the three ninja made their way up to Kai's room. Guards were everywhere around the compound — both inside and out — so they had to sneak into Kai's room using the balconies outside each window. Lloyd and Cole both easily swung from balcony to balcony, slipping into Kai's room quietly under the shadow of night. But just as Jay grabbed on to the bottom of Kai's railing, the woman staying in the room next to Kai's stepped onto her balcony!

Jay yelped. Kai tried hard not to look down at his friend.

The woman — Skylor — turned to Kai and asked, "What was that you said?"

Kai shrugged. "I said '*Yelp!* What a **beautiful night**.'"

Below the balcony, Jay struggled to hold on. But he knew he couldn't get caught. Not by Chen's guards *or* the other competitors. Either one was sure to turn him in to Chen for breaking rules.

The woman and Kai continued to chat for a while, while Jay grew more and more frustrated. Jay was sure that Kai was trying to torture him by forcing him to hang on for as long as he did. Finally, Kai said good night, and Skylor went back inside her suite.

Jay swung up onto Kai's balcony and griped, "You just *had* to leave me hanging."

Kai grinned. Inside, the other ninja took in Kai's suite. "Nice digs," said Jay.

"I know!" said Cole. "His room is so much nicer than mine. Look, chocolate-covered peas. I love these!" He grabbed a handful, then jumped onto Kai's bed. "And look how soft your pillows are! Mine are made of rock. What a crock."

Suddenly, the bed flipped over — with Cole **inside it**!

The other three didn't notice he was gone.

"So, like we planned," said Lloyd. "Tonight, we stick together."

Suddenly, the bed rotated back around and Cole was on top of it again. No one had even realized he'd been gone. "Uh, guys? This bed is —"

"Cole, I get it," snapped Kai. "You like my bed. Would you stop playing around?"

Cole nodded. He looked to the drawing of the snake symbol Kai had seen near his bed, then back at his friends. He grinned widely.

"I think I know how we can search the island!" he exclaimed.

He told the others his plan, and a few moments later, all four ninja were squeezed into Kai's bed.

"You're right," said Jay. "The pillows are soft."

Lloyd looked annoyed. "I feel ridiculous. Is this a joke?"

Cole poked at the mattress, looking for something. "I must've done something to trigger it before. I was lying here, then I stretched —"

Cole reached his arm up and felt around. He pressed on the pillows, and on the wall near the snake symbol. Suddenly, his finger hit a small hidden button on the headboard, and the bed flipped over!

The four ninja fell out of the bed and thudded loudly on the ground of a dark tunnel. They had found some sort of hidden chamber below Kai's room!

"A secret passageway," said Jay, eyes wide. "Cool!"

Kai nodded. "Nice work, Cole." He considered something for a moment. He thought about how guards had seemed to just *appear* when they were near the waterfall, close to the symbol — but where had they come from? Then he thought about how Karlof had mysteriously **disappeared** into the trapdoor in the ground after the battle the night before. He considered their search from earlier in the day, and how they'd found no leads while looking for Zane. Suddenly, he had a new idea. What if the mysterious symbol was a sign of trapdoors leading **into the island**?

"Guys?" Kai said. "Maybe Zane's not *on* the island, but *in* it."

The four ninja smiled at one another as they all realized the same thing: They had just found their first real lead in the search for Zane. It was time to search underground!

The next stage of the ninja's adventure was officially *on*.

NINJAGO™
Masters of Spinjitzu

L NEW EPISODES 2015

CARTOON NETWORK